2

Danny Looks for Abby

written and photographed
by
Mia Coulton

One day I went
to play with Abby.
The gate was open.

Abby was not in her yard.
She was gone.

I looked in the shed.

She was not there.

I looked behind the shed.

She was not there.

Where was Abby?

I looked behind

the garbage can.

She was not there.

I looked in the bushes.

She was not there.

Where was Abby?

I barked and barked.

She did not come.

I could not find Abby.

She was gone!

I walked home.

I was very sad.

I could not find Abby.

Where was Abby?

Abby was gone.

Then I saw Abby!

She was at my gate.

I could not find Abby

because she

came to play

in my yard!